THE COWBOY
AND THE
BLACK-EYED PEA

THE COWBOY
AND THE
BLACK-EYED PEA

by Tony Johnston
illustrated by Warren Ludwig

PaperStar

The Putnam & Grosset Group

For all my friends and relations
of the great Lone Star state—T.J.

With love to Doris and Stan, to Kris and Debra,
and to grandmother.—W.L.

Text copyright © 1992 by Tony Johnston.
Illustrations copyright © 1992 by Warren Ludwig.
All rights reserved. This book, or parts thereof, may not be reproduced
in any form without permission in writing from the publisher.
A PaperStar Book, published in 1996 by The Putnam & Grosset Group,
345 Hudson Street, New York, NY 10014.
PaperStar and the PaperStar logo are trademarks of The Putnam Berkley Group, Inc.
Originally published in 1992 by G. P. Putnam's Sons, New York.
Published simultaneously in Canada.
Manufactured in China
Library of Congress Cataloging-in-Publication Data
Johnston, Tony. The cowboy and the black-eyed pea/
by Tony Johnston; illustrated by Warren Ludwig. p.   cm.
Summary: In this adaptation of "The Princess and the Pea," the wealthy daughter of
a Texas rancher devises a plan to find a real cowboy among her many suitors.
[1. Fairy Tales. 2. Cowboys—Fiction. 3. Texas—Fiction. 4. West (U.S.)—Fiction.]
I. Ludwig, Warren, ill. II. Title.   PZ8.J494Co 1992 [E]—dc20 91-21606 CIP AC
ISBN 0-698-11356-X
7 9 10 8 6

5508

Out where coyotes serenade the moon and sagebrush grays the land, there lived a young woman of bodacious beauty. Her name was Farethee Well.

Her daddy was fixing to leave her all his worldly goods—a fine herd of longhorns, a corral full of horses, and the biggest spread in the great state of Texas.

On his deathbed he said to Farethee Well, "Come and sit by my side."
So she did.

"Honey," he whispered, "when I'm gone and you're rich, men will flock here like flies to pralines, seeking your hand in marriage. Find a *real* cowboy who'll love you for yourself, not just for your longhorn herd."

Sure enough, quick as you can say "set another place at table," cowboys from hither and yon came seeking Farethee Well's hand.

Farethee Well had herself a fine problem. How could she tell a *real* cowboy from a fake? She thought on what course to take. Then she recalled her daddy's words: "A *real* cowboy is known for his sensitivity. At the least touch he'll bruise like the petals of a desert rose."

Knowing that, she devised a plan. Whenever a caller came to ask for her hand, she'd slip an itty-bitty black-eyed pea beneath his saddle blanket. Then she'd send him out on the range. Should he return fresh as a Texas morning, he was a fake. A *real* cowboy would be sorely troubled by that pea.

One day such a caller rode in. He was tall as a tree, with a mustache as big as tarnation. He wore spurs the size of tambourines.

"Marry me, ma'am," he said. "And I'll run this place for you."

Without delay she put him to the test.

"Just ride the range today," said Farethee Well. "When you return, I'll give you my reply."

Then, unnoticed, she slipped an itty-bitty black-eyed pea beneath his saddle blanket.

The cowboy set out, mustache a-jouncing, spurs a-jingling. All day he roamed the spread that he thought would soon be his. Then he returned, fresh as a Texas morning and prideful as a rooster.

"Marry me, ma'am," he said, swinging down from the saddle.

"No sir," said Farethee Well. "You're not a *real* cowboy at all."

"How can you tell?" he hissed, mean as a snake.

"I have my ways. *Adios*."

Well, he'd never been adiosed like that before.

"HOGS!" he roared, stomping his feet. *"I didn't want to marry you anyhow!"*

And he cut on out of there.

Come daylight, another caller appeared, bristling with pistols and brag.
He wore tooled leather boots, an overgrown neckerchief, and fringes galore.
Real swagger clothes.

"Marry me, ma'am," he said. "And I'll run this spread for you."

Farethee Well figured he didn't know the front end of a horse from the rear.
Still, she put him to the test.

With the itty-bitty black-eyed pea hidden beneath his saddle, the cowboy set out, neckerchief a-flying, fringes a-flapping. At the end of the day he returned, fresh as a Texas morning and swelled with swagger like a horned toad.

"Marry me, ma'am," he said, swinging down from the saddle.

"No sir," said Farethee Well. "You're not a *real* cowboy at all."

"How do you know?" He glared with a look hard as petrified grits.

"I have my ways. *Adios.*"

Well, he'd never been adiosed like that before.

"BEANS!" he roared. *"I didn't want to marry you anyhow!"*

And he cut on out of there.

So it was. Cowboys came and went. But none was a *real* cowboy—not a one.

One day a rushing rain fell down so fast it like to float the ranch house away. In the midst of the downpour, a young man knocked at the door. Rivulets of water gushed from his boots and over the porch like quicksilver streams. They ran so hard and fast it seemed he was the very *cause* of the storm.

"Mind if I sit out the storm here?" he asked.

He did not ask for her hand. But something about him gave her a notion.
So she said, "My longhorns don't much like rain. Would you ride out and
check on them? Then come right on back."

"No trouble at all," said the cowboy.

While he was pouring the rain from his hat, Farethee Well tucked the
itty-bitty black-eyed pea under his saddle blanket.

Scarcely had the cowboy reached the fence, when the pea commenced to work at him. He touched the reins and headed back. He swung down and checked the saddle. Something was almighty wrong with it, but he couldn't figure what.

"Ma'am," he called to Farethee Well. "I believe I need another saddle blanket."

Farethee Well fetched another blanket. He piled it on top of the first one. Then he set out once more.

As he rode along, he twisted and twitched. The saddle squeaked and creaked. Despite his squirming, he could find no comfort.

So, again, the cowboy returned.

"Ma'am," he called. "Could you spare another saddle blanket? Something's surely worked its way under my saddle. But I can't locate the culprit."

Farethee Well fetched another blanket, which the cowboy piled on top of the others. And he set out once more.

Time and again he retraced his steps. Time and again Farethee Well gave him more blankets, till he was sitting on no fewer than fifty saddle blankets, all stacked up like flapjacks. Though the view was fine from that perch, the itty-bitty black-eyed pea was just a-working and a-rubbing and causing him no end of pain.

The cowboy gritted his teeth against it. Though he sorely needed more blankets, he thought, "This time I'll not go back. I've got a job to do." And he rode out toward the herd.

The rain kept coming down. Lightning sizzled across the sky. Then a boom of thunder spooked the longhorns something awful. They set up a fearsome bawling and cut loose like a runaway locomotive.

There seemed no way to control them. The cowboy and his horse were wedged between the cattle. So, of course, they took off too!

Ooooo-*weeeee*! It was a painful ride, jolting up and down on that itty-bitty black-eyed pea.

It was a dangerous ride too. Like as not, the rampaging longhorns would squash both man and horse.

But the cowboy had a stroke of luck. Back at the ranch, Farethee Well had heard the thundering herd.

"Stampede!" she thought. And she raced to slow it down.

Right off, she saw the cowboy caught in the middle, high atop his flapjack pile of saddle blankets, unable to reach his stirrups. Even above the bawling cattle, she heard his groans of pain—all produced by that vexatious black-eyed pea. It hurt so, he like to died.

Farethee Well lit out to save him. She cut right into the running herd.
"SKEDADDLE!" she whooped. Sure enough, those longhorns skedaddled
every whichaway.

Though the cowboy was saved, a more pitiful sight you've rarely seen. By now he didn't look much like a *real* cowboy. But Farethee Well knew he was.

"Howdy," he said, attempting to smile.

"Howdy," said Farethee Well. "You don't look so good."

"Fact is, ma'am, setting on this saddle is like setting on sheer stone."

He eased down from the saddle. Farethee Well checked under the pile of blankets.

"I declare!" she cried, fetching out something not much bigger than a flea. "It's nothing at all. Just this itty-bitty black-eyed pea."

"Well, I'll be," said the cowboy.

He was truly amazed.

This time Farethee Well never said adios. For soon they were married, and they set off on a wedding trip.

The stars that night were big and bright as they saddled their horses and headed out. In front of them shone a full-blown Texas moon. Behind them, a full-grown Texas mule ambled along, piled high with saddle blankets—in case the need should arise.